# Little Wolf's Diary of DARING Deeds

IAN WHYBROW

Illustrated by Tony Ross

HarperCollins *Children's Books*

First published in Great Britain by Collins in 1996
This edition published by HarperCollins Children's Books in 2012
HarperCollins Children's Books is an imprint of HarperCollins*Publishers* Ltd
77-85 Fulham Palace Road, Hammersmith, London, W6 8JB

1



ISBN 978 0 00 745856 1



Printed and bound in England
by Clays Ltd, St Ives plc

MIX
Paper from
responsible sources
FSC C007454

FSC™ is a non-profit international organisation established to promote
the responsible management of the world's forests. Products carrying the
FSC label are independently certified to assure consumers that they come
from forests that are managed to meet the social, economic and
ecological needs of present and future generations,
and other controlled sources.

Find out more about HarperCollins and the environment at
**www.harpercollins.co.uk/green**

To my own daring-deeders:
Ted and Amelie, Ella and Fifi

HAMNEESIA
SPOOKE
MT. FARVIEW
WHITE
GRIM MOUNTAINS
MT. SKYWARD
MT. TESTER
BROKEN TOOTH CAVES
BEASTSHIRE
N
W
S
E
DARK HILLS
WINDY RIDGE
FRETNIN FOREST
CUNNING COLLEGE
ADVENTURE ACADEMY
LAKE LEMMING
RIVER RIGGLY
SCAL

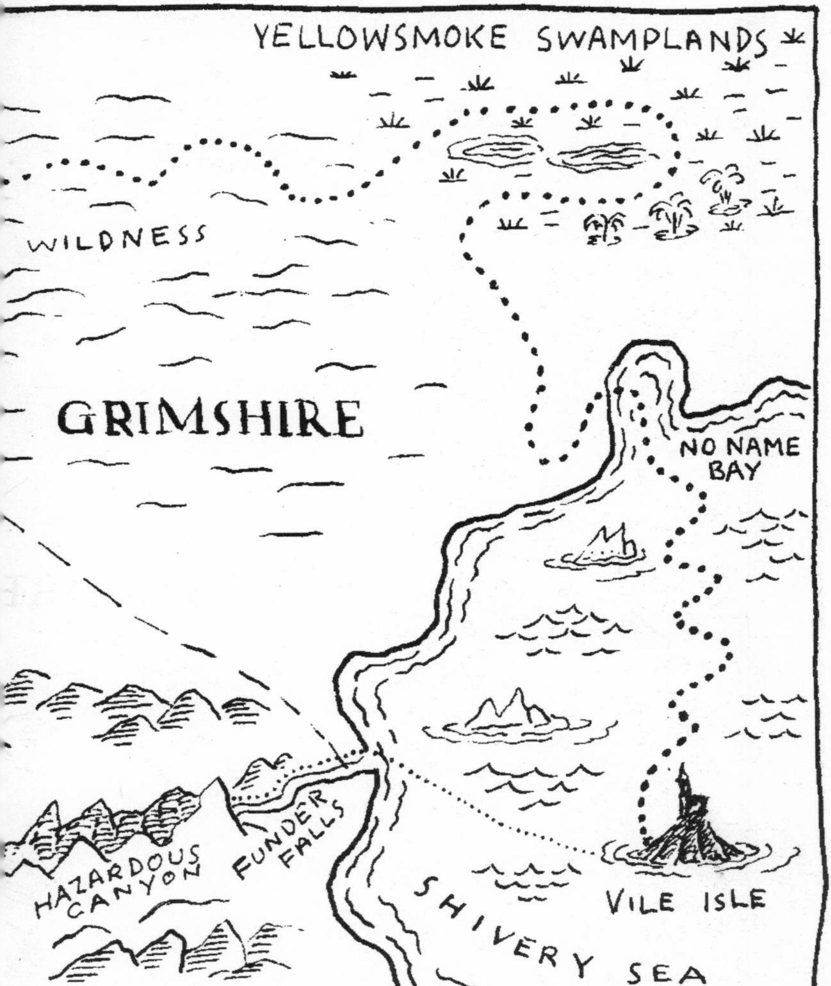

YELLOWSMOKE SWAMPLANDS

WILDNESS

GRIMSHIRE

NO NAME BAY

HAZARDOUS CANYON

FUNDER FALLS

SHIVERY SEA

VILE ISLE

: 5 CROWS FEET - 1 MILE

FOR DARING DEEDERS
FRETTNIN FOREST, BEASTSHIRE
HEADS: ~~BIGBAD WOLF, ESQ~~
LITTLE WOLF AND YELLER WOLF, ESQS

↑ Better, eh?

Dear Mum and Dad,

Please please PLEEEZ come and move in here, you said you would. Because my cuz Yeller is coming soonly to be a Head with me. Then we can get some pupils and start up Adventure Academy at last!!

I cannot wait hardly. I have found bags and bags of gold that Uncle Bigbad hid. That means I am RICH!! So we are going to have the best fun school ever. Also we are going to buy the best adventures in the world and put them in our playground. Then we can do daring deeds all the time, arrrooo!

Go on, I want you to come so you can be proud of me. Dad can retire from his work at Fang and Mauler and put his paws up. I have made the cellar all nice and smelly for you just like the Lair, so you can be happy hibernators for ever after.

Tell Smellybreff, yes, he can be a teacher because he is my baby bruv, but remember, me and Yeller are pack leaders, so no moaning.

Yours hurryupply,

Little

PS I am sending you some more gold so you can come by helicopter.

Dear Mum and Dad,

Posh paper, eh?

Big gales in the night. Tell the helicopter pilot I am a bit wurrid about him not seeing which part of the forest to come down in. So I have done HELLO HELLY LAND ON YOUR BELLY on a big mat for him.

Still no Yeller, boo shame, where is he? I wish he would hurry up because his ideas are just the best. Also I need him to help me with adverts for our school. I did one today but it is rubbish, look:

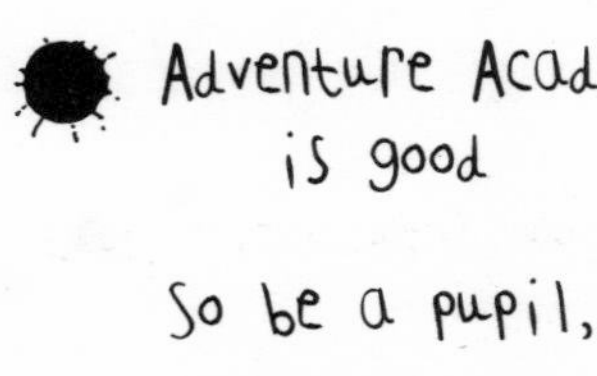

Well it is quite good rhyming. But shame I forgot to say about having fun and getting Daring Deed badges.

I 'spect Yeller is coming by slowcoach (get it?).

From your

Littly

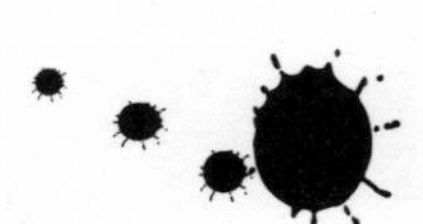

Dear Mum and Dad,

Arrrroooo! The postman came today with a big parcel saying, "Phew, heavy, hint hint." So I said to put it down in the hall and filled up his hands with gold.

He said, "Cor thanks, Master L, you are a lot nicer than your Uncle Bigbad. When he was here being Head of Cunning College for Brute Beasts, he used to eat postmen. He was a big horrible miser, he was. They say he had bags and bags of gold buried all over the place, but he never spent one penny, not like you. Good thing he went off bang if you ask me."

I gave him a small wolfly nip and a grrr for cheek and off he went happy and rich.

All of a suddenly the parcel went crickle crackle rip. Then out jumped a something saying a huge big

RRRRRRRRAAAAAAAAAAHHHH!

and making my heart hop like frogs. And what was it? It was Yeller! I was so pleased to see his funny pointy face and my trick arrow through his head. And so good to hear his voice again, yelling, "HELLO LICKLE, HOW DID YOU LIKE MY TRICK PARCEL?"

Who else would think of a clever trick joke like posting yourself? Plus he brought me a posh present, a book for writing our adventures in. I am calling it *My Diary of Daring Deeds*, so 1 day all our grandcubs will read it and go, "Oo look, so brave," ect.

Yours proudly,

Little

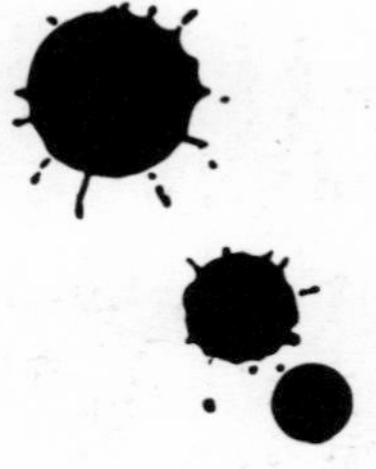

Dear Mum and Dad,

Your crool letter you sent yesterday says you will not move in here now. Whyo Y have you changed your minds? Is it because Uncle Bigbad went off bang and Dad blames me? I bet it is. But I *told* him not to scoff all my bakebeans with a shovel. He just did not listen, being such a greedyguts.

PLEEEZ change your minds back again.

Yours upsettly,

Little

Dear Mum and Dad,

Murkshire is nice, yes, and the Lair is cosy, yes. But you will soon like Beastshire when you see it. Also Frettnin Forest is just the scaryest, Dad will love it.

But you say you think my plans are 2 showoff and cubbish. Dad says he does not agree with Adventure Playgrounds. He is so oldfashy. Because when you are rich and modern, you can buy adventures and be Daring Deeders at home. No need to go a long way for them. Or get killed, ect. See?

Yours pantingly,

Littly

Dear M and D,

Just to show you what you are missing. Look at this advert. Yeller found it in *Wolf Weekly* yesterday.

**MISTER MARVO'S INSTANT ADVENTURES**

**SCARY BUT SAFE**

**ALSO WINTERPROOF AND UNBREAKABLE BY BRUTE BEASTS**

*DEMONSTRATIONS BY APPOINTMENT*

See? It is brilliant. I am writing for a Mister Marvo appointment today! So go on, Mum and Dad, get on the helicopter quick!

Yours reallywantingly,

Littley

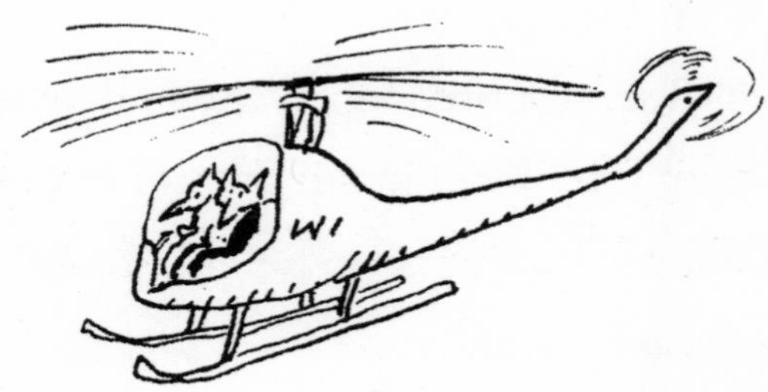

Dear Mum and Dad,

Yes I was surprised when the helicopter landed and baby bruv Smellybreff got out but not you. Yes I got your note off him, no he did not do a sick down his new sailor suit.

Yes I made sure he did not leave his ted in the helicopter. Yes I do know teddy is his best friend.

Yes I do understand that you are trusting me with your small darling baby pet till Springtime comes. Yes I know you will go RAVING MAD if I let anything bad happen to him.

Yes I promise I will keep writing and say if Smellybreff gets homesick or bangs his tiny nose, ect.

Yes you are right, it is furfluffingly chilly here and all the chestnuts have fallen.

I hope you enjoy your long winter zizz without us. When are you starting xactly? Also, are you sure you do not want to have your tiny Smells tucked up cosy in your bed?

Yours ??ly,

Little

Dear Mum and Dad,

Smells has been here 2 days now. He has been stupid and whiny and keeps messing my things up. Also, he will not call me and Yeller sir, even though we are Heads.

He is hopeless at Schools and playing teachers. But 1 thing he likes a lot is gold. I bought him a metal detector yesterday and off he went hunting for more of Uncle Bigbad's gold. He found 4 more bags. Now he wants a safe with a big key, PLUS combination lock.

Yours a bit feduppply,

Little

Dear Mum and Dad,

Guess what! A letter came from Mr Marvo today. He is coming soonly to tell us all about Instant Adventures for our playground, arrroooo! Yeller has got some brilliant BIG IDEAS for what we want, gokarts, motorbikes, roller-coasters, zipwire, dodgems, wall-of-death, helter skelter, parachute-jumper, arcade racing machines, ect! What is rubbish about that, Dad? Answer, nothing.

No winter zizzes for us cubs, we are much 2 excited.

Yours cannotwaitly,

L

Dear Mum and Dad,

Smells wants me to send you a pic of his new safe so here it is.

Also he says har har he knows the number to open it but not me. So cubbish.

Your big boy,

L

Dear Mum and Dad,

Smells is OK today but a bit goldfeverish. He howled his head off till I gave him all my gold to put in his safe. Plus all the new bags he keeps finding with his metal detector.

This is what he does all the time. 1st he piles up gold in sixes (he only knows up to 6). Then he kisses each pile and puts them in his safe. Then he locks up. Then he whispers through the keyhole, "Night night darlings, sleepy tight. Daddy soon find you some more nice shiny friends to chink with."

What do you think about this?

Askingly

Little Wolf

Dear Mum and Dad,

Just got your letter saying let him get on with it. Good because I have.

From your not so wurrid,

Little

Dear Mum and Dad,

Good thing Adventure Acad is snowproof. Outside is all white, Yeller's worst thing. It made his voice lose some of its loudness. He said to me, "OH NO, LICKLE, NOW MISTER MARVO WON'T COME! THE SNOW IS TERRIBLE!"

But he did, he came by snowmobile! It is a big shiny one with a propeller behind. Plus cosy glass cabin in front. Mister M is tall and smart with his black coat sticking out at the back and a big fuzzy beard. It comes right up to his glinty eyes. His voice is a sleepy one and his smell is like pepper and his eyebrows are red and bristly.

After tea he showed me and Yeller some plans of Instant Adventures. He does nice curly capitals and he is a good colourinner. But plans are hard to understand for small cubs. Never mind, because Mister Marvo is so clever. He says, "Believe me, my boys, these are the most marvellous, most modernest adventures money can buy! They cost a lot, but remember, they are all under 1 winterproof dome. So you can have the thrills without the chills."

Yeller said, "ARRRROOOO! BECAUSE SNOW IS MY WORST THING, IT GIVES ME THE TREMBLES. BUT NOW, GUESS WHAT LICKLE, WE CAN HAVE A GO WITHOUT THE SNOW!!"

See what you are missing?

Yours xcitedly

L

Dear M and D,

Smells thinks Mister Marvo is brilliant. He has let him share his dorm, also shown him his ted and his safe even!

Me and Yeller are not jealous because now we can get on playing Bossy Heads and Daring Deeders by ourself. Important for the practiss. And tomorrow we choose our Instant Adventures, arrrroooo!

Yours thrilly,

Dear Mum and Dad,

Plan plan plan is what me and Yeller and Mister Marvo are up to, phew. Smells will not help, he only likes counting gold.

These are our best IAs so far (short for Instant Adventures).

PIRATE RAIDERS

SPACE RANGERS

FIERCE FIGHTERS

NIGHT ON MONSTER MOUNTAIN

TARZAN ZIPWIRES

Mister Marvo said did we want BANGS-U-LIKE ADVENTURE which is like a forest? You creep through it and loads of pretend hunters jump out and shoot their guns at you. Yeller said "GOOD IDEA, I LOVE LOUDNESS."

But I said, "No, that is enough IAs for now."

I did not want to say I am v scared of bangs, but all of a suddenly, Mister Marvo said softly, "Look deep into my eyes, my boy, and tell me. Are bangs your worst thing?" Just then Yeller did a loud sneeze, lucky for me. It made me jump plus it stopped me giving away my secret.

So Mister Marvo said, "Well done, my boy, it is plain that you do not fear bangs. Naturally you are thinking of your pupils, who will not all be as fearless as you. By the way, the Instant Adventures you have selected will cost 3 wheelbarrowsful of gold, paid in advance."

I said, "What, before you build anything? Good joke har har."

Then Mister Marvo got quite snarly. It made his beard slip a bit and show his sharp teeth. But quick as a chick he hid them, saying he would build us a nice X-ample of his marvellous work, a TARZAN ZIPWIRE. Good, eh?

Yours proudly,

The Owner2be

Dear M and D,

Smells is still OK but a bit jealous and fidgety because of Mister Marvo doing planning with us. Yesterday he kept climbing on top of his safe and falling off. Just so we would stick plasters on him.

Then Yeller had a BIG IDEA. He made Smells a tape of gold going chinkle chinkle. Now it is 1 of his best things. He sits and listens to it all the time with his Earpod on.

See, we are looking after him still.

Your trusted

Little

Dear Mum and Dad,

Today Mister Marvo put up the mini Tarzan Zipwire in our dorm to show us.

I said to Yeller, "Yeller, what do you think?" He said to me, "I THINK IT IS A BIT RUBBISH, LICKLE." Mister Marvo said to Yeller, "With respect, my boy, Master Little is the true owner here. I advise you to keep silent." He gave Yeller a deep look in the eyes and guess what, Yeller said, "OF COURSE, GREAT SIR, I WILL OBEY." It is so hard to say no to Mister Marvo.

True the zipwire is a bit smaller than we hoped. More washingliney than Tarzanny. But still, we had 236 goes on it. It is good the way it makes your eyes water and blows your fur back. Also you go dong off the tyres at the end and that takes some daringness.

Mister Marvo says not to be wurrid, it is just an Example IA. When we pay him, he will build a huge big scary real 1 over a stream with pretend crocs going snap. Oo-er!

Yours phewly,

L

Dear Mum and Dad,

Sorry to hear about your blizzard blowing. Another white whisker day here also. So have a nice hibernate and see you in Springtime. Us cubs are much 2 busy for long zizzing.

Yes I will write down all news but not send it, just save it for when you wake up. I will put it all in my Daring Deed book that Yeller gave me. No I will not disturb, only in Emerjuncy. Like if any badness happens to my baby bruv. Which it will not, Dad, because yes I do remember what you get like when you go RAVING MAD.

Yours nightnightnightnightnightnightly ect (get it?),

L

Dear Hibernaties,

Mister Marvo is still here. He is doing lots of hard complications and guess what he says?
He says, "My boys, you now have my personal guarantee as a marvoman and inventor, that your Instant Adventure Playground, the finest in the world, will be ready by the end of the month! My team of busy beavers will start work as soon as I give the word."

Arrrroooo! Time to get our pupils together. Must think up a good advert.

Yours thinkingly,

Little

Dear Hiberzizzers,

Smells has gone barmy about Yeller's chinkle tape, he loves it, kiss kiss!

He has stopped talking to everybody. He only likes staying in his dorm guarding his safe, so he can count up gold, plus listening to his chinkle tape on his Walkwolf. I think Mister Marvo is a bit upset. He keeps saying "My boy, this won't do at all. Won't you look deep into my eyes and say 'Yes, Mister Marvo, I am your best pal?'" But Smells just turns up his Earpod and sings, "Chinkle chinkle little gold, you are wot I like to hold."

Yours reportingly,

L Wolf (Head)

~~OTTER~~ BALLOON,

Hot air, sorry

*above Frettnin Forest*

Dear M and D,

Yeller has thought of an advert for getting pupils, it is just the best! That is Y I am writing this in a balloon!!! It has the shape of Adventure Acad, but with a basket hanging under.

Me and Yeller are floating over Frettnin Forest. We have got cardboard loudshouters and this is what we shout for our advert (Yeller made it up but I wrote it down):

"Ahoy ahoy, brute beasts!! Do you like adventures? Then come to our school and have some. Yes, come to Adventure Academy! It is the big place they used to call Cunning College. Mister Bigbad Wolf was the Head. But not now, he went off bang and died. So all is changed, no need to fear and fret. Little and Yeller Wolf are the new Heads. So come, be our pupils! Try our new adventure playground. It is the BEST FUN EVER! Plus you get Daring Deed Awards. Arrroooo!"

Yours skyhighly,

L

Dear Mum and Dad,

Bit wurrid about baby bruv again. It is gold gold gold all the time with him now.

I know you think he has not got goldfever. But last night he gave his precious ted a bath in gold! I fear he is a bit gone in the brane because everybody knows Smells hates baths.

Also, now he has locked Mister Marvo out of his dorm and will not speak to him at all.

Yours ahwelly,

Little

Dear Zizzy Parents,

Good news, our balloon advert worked. Now we have got 1 pupil, Arrrooo! He was left on our doorstep. He is a small crow with not much feathers, v shy with a label on. He does not say much, only Ark. This is what his label said:

STUBBS CROW
TOO FRIT TO FLY
BUT GOOD AT
BEAKWORK

Yours readingly,

L Wolf (Head)

Dear Parents,

Some cubs would look at Stubbs and say, "Hmm nice snack", but not me and Yeller. We want to teach him not eat him.

Yeller is good at being a Head. He shouts cheery things like, "HELLO STUBBY! WELCOME TO ADVENTURE ACADEMY. ME AND MY CO-HEAD LICKLE WILL SOON TEACH YOU HOW TO BE A HIGH FLYER AND DARING DEEDER LIKE US. BEAK UP! NO NEED TO BE A SCAREDYCROW!"

Also we have let him nest in the fireplace in the hall with his head up the chimney to feel more homely.

Yours nicely,

L

Dear Parents,

Mister Marvo keeps asking and asking for 1 wheelbarrow of gold to show we are good sports. Just to start up, he says. It is hard saying no to him but Yeller says we must try and keep our firmness up, saying, "NO MEANS NO!" with loud grrrs like Dad.

Also, if he talks softly to us we cross our eyes and go blah doo dum diddle inside our heads.

I have just heard Mister Marvo going grumblymumbly up to bed. I wish he would hurry up and bring his busy beavers to start work on the Adventure Playground, then he can have his gold.

Yours keentostartly,

L

*Morning*

Dear Mum and Dad,

Good thing I am writing this in my Diary of Daring Deeds and not posting this yet. Because I think you might go a bit mad.

It is just that Mister Marvo has stolen all my gold and cubnapped Smells, sorry.

Your other boy,

L Wolf

PS Still, do not get wurrid, by the time you read this, everything will be Ok.
Probly.

*Later*

Dear Mum and Dad,

Help, we still do not know what to do! Because 1) the snow is tall as cubs, 2) Yeller is scared of snow. Also how can we catch up Mister Marvo in his fast snowmobile? Oo-er.

Just back from a clue hunt. Near the front door we found:

1 top hat

1 bushy beard

1 long coat with red tailhairs all up the back inside.

What do they mean?

Yours stumpedly,

Little

*Much Later*

Dear M and D,

Oh no, guess what, Mister Marvo is not really a marvoman and inventor at all! No, he is a cunning fox and a clever dizgizzer (cannot spell it). And his really truly name is Mister Twister the Fox! He was Uncle Bigbad's crime partner, remember? Also he made me work for him at Borderlands Market 1 time when I was lost. Fancy me not knowing him by his pepper smell plus his sneaky questions like are bangs my worst thing? Plus saying MY BOY THIS and MY BOY THAT all the time!

Also Smells left us a clue on paper, but it is rubbish because he can only do ABC. This is it:

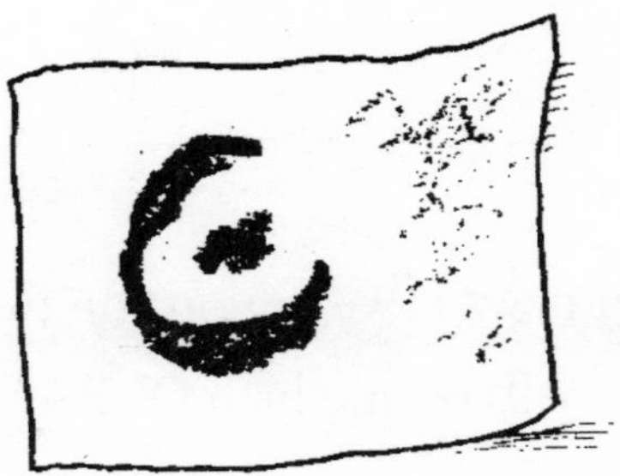

Do not fret and fear, I spect Yeller will think up a rescue Idea soon.

Yours onyourmarksly,

*Middle of Frettnin Forest*
*(small gap in)*

Dear M and D,

The cheery news is we are on the trail of Mister Twister and Smells on my bike (Yeller's idea, quicker than paws).

Yeller has got the Snowtrembles v bad. So his voice has gone all quiet. This morning he whispered to me, "LICKLE, THE SNOW HAS TOOK MY VOICE."

I said, "Yeller, that is an old wolf's tale. The snow does not want voices."

He is still wurrid but brave. Also Stubbs did not want to stay behind so we tucked him in the rucksack. It is a bit like flying for him with his head sticking out, only not 2 highupp.

We have plenty of snacks, tent, torches, ect. Also Yeller has brought Smells' clue, plus his kite with the yellow wolf eyes and strong string as Rescue Kit. Now we are having a short rest in a small gap in Frettnin Forest. 2 cold stars are lighting this letter, maybe 3, brrr. I think we have come 4 or 5 miles.

If we keep on the snowmobile track, fine. If not, whoops plop, where are we? Answer, under the snow digging.

Yours searchingly,

Little

PS We will rescue Smells quick as we can, so Dad, do not go RAVING MAD.

*Near South Shore of Lake Lemming*

Dear Mum and Dad,

What a rooty nightride we had through Frettnin Forest with our torches going flash. The tent was so heavy on the back of the bike, also it pressed on the brakes and made us go slower. But all is not sadness and sore botts because we have got to the south shore of Lake Lemming. Now v late but we can rest. The tent is up and a snuggly fit with 3 of us in.

Yeller and me had hedgehog and cowparsley soup for a warmupp. I said to Stubbs, "Do crows like chocklit earwigs?" He said "Ark! Ark-zactly!" his 1st words. He is a bit shy for Rescue work.

Yours sorebottly,

L

*Still in tent*

*Early morning-time*

Dear Mum and Dad,

I cannot sleep because of thinking Y did Mister Twister take Smells with him? Is it...

A) because he likes small pests or

B) because Smells loves gold so much he will not say the combination of the safe?

I bet it is B. And I bet when they are faraway, Mister Twister will take the Earpod off Smells's ears. Then he will say softly, "Look deep deep into my eyes, my boy, and tell me the number of your safe." Not fair, because Mister Twister is such a cunning crook and cubnapper but Dad will still go raving mad at *me* for letting a bad thing happen to Smells.

Your tuffluckly,

Little

*Lake Lemming north shore*
*morning*

Dear Mum and Dad,

Yeller and me were all down and dumpy after only a small zizz. I was on the back of the bike because it was Yeller's turn to pedal. He said whisperly, "PHEW LICKLE, THIS IS 2 HARD FOR ME. I WISH THERE WAS A MORE EASY WAY TO CATCH THAT SNOWMOBILE."

Just then Stubbs tapped me on the head and pointed his beak northly.

I said, "Do you mean go straightly, the crow way?" He said, "Ark." I said, "But that is straight over the lake." He said, "Ark-zactly!".

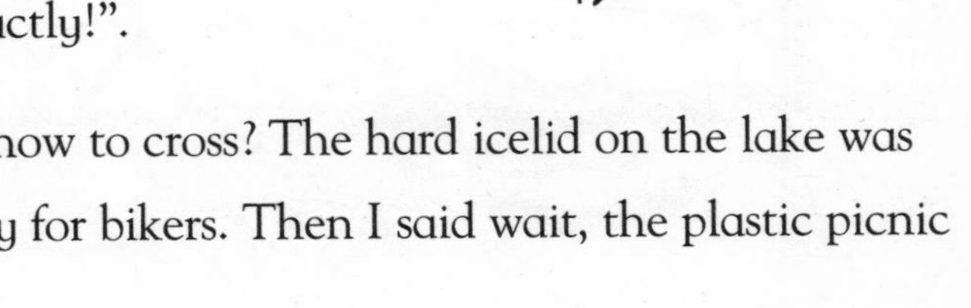

But how to cross? The hard icelid on the lake was 2 skiddy for bikers. Then I said wait, the plastic picnic plates!

We got off the bike and Yeller and me tied 1 plate on each back paw. Then on to the lake we stepped. “Hold tight, Stubbs!” I said and off we went, skaty skate! 1st we went

FFFSHH-BONK, OO MY NOSE!

FFFSHH-BONK, OO MY TAIL!

But then Stubby spread out his wings for the balance and off I sailed, smooth as smooth! That

gave Yeller the Idea to use his kite, so no more falling down for us. Oo what a thrilly feeling and FREEE! Better than silly old Tarzan Zipwires that cost barrows of money! Also, a good Daring Deed for my Diary, tick. ✓

1 bad thing about picnic plates is they are brakeless. So we met the north shore in a sudden way. Lucky there was a soft snowpile to land in, phew.

We brushed ourselves off and guess what we saw right away, snowmobile tracks going hillward, arrrooo! So that Mister Twister better watch out, we know he has gone to Windy Ridge!

Yours sherlockly,

Little

PS Also we found a small heap of grey fluffy stuff. Not sure what it is but Stubbs has kept it for a cosy nest-liner.

*Windy Ridge*
*Late afternoon*

Dear Mum and Dad,

After a short rest, we all did jumping for the warmness. Also made a fire for toasting cheese (Stubbs's best snack). Crunchy shrewbar for me, hmmm nice, then quickmarch, back doing Rescuing.

All afternoon we hiked pantingly. At last Stubbs tapped my head and then his beak pointed over the hill to Windy Ridge. Aha, there was the snowmobile right up there, with Mister Twister plus Smells tied up! Yeller said (small trembly voice), "LET'S CREEP UP CLOSE, LICKLE, THEN WAIT TILL DEEP DARK. THEN JUMP ON THAT FOX AND CAPTURE HIM!"

We got on our bellyfur in the cold snow, doing the wolfcrawl. Poor Yeller, it was so bad for his Snowtrembles. But Stubbs helped him keep up his cheeryness whispering, "Ark! Ark-cellent! Ark-cellent!" all the way up to the top.

We waited and waited, quiet as catbreath till the dark was deep. Then one paw at a time, careful not to make the snow squeak:

We got out our torches

And we snuck up behind Mister Twister

And tied him up quick!

Only it was not Mister Twister, ect, only cardboard cutouts and a note.

**My boys, you can never hope to catch me. It is only a matter of time before the Brat tells me the combination of the safe. Then I shall release him. So give up and go home. Otherwise you will put the Brat in danger and you will face some VERY LOUD BANGS. You have been warned. Give up now, signed Mister Twister.**

Yours trickedly,

Little

*Outside Broken Tooth Caves*

Dear Mum and Dad,

Today was just the worst. Mister Twister had tons of time to escape across the Dark Hills, plus get here to Broken Tooth Caves.

Before we started, Yeller said, "BANGS ARE YOUR WORST THING, LICKLE. DO YOU WANT TO GIVE UP?"
I said, "Snow is your worst thing. Do you want to give up?" We both said, "No!" and kept going. So now Mister Twister will most probly join up with some outlaws in a gang and bash us with loud snowballs.

The Dark Hills were v cold and horrible with snow feather flakes coming down. So no more snowmobile tracks. Then down flew that sharp stuff, not snow, more like grit or stingflies but no taste. Sleet is it?

This is a bad place. So many caves, all joined together like ratruns. Just the lurky sort that outlaws and bears like, oo-er!

We have picked a good dry cave for our nightlair. Hope we can keep safe.

Your tracky boy,

Little

Dear Mum and Dad,

Today we did a Daring Deed with a lion in it. Yes a real mountain 1!

We slept a safe night but boiling up bat soup for breakfast was 2 much of a danger-tempter. Because a hungry old mountain lion came sniffing! Stubbs smelt his catsmell before me even, and saved us from ambush. He went, "Ark! Ark-shun stations! Ark-shun stations!" We just had time to run behind the fire. All of a suddenly, we saw his eyes, then his teeth, then his blue cap and waistcoat. He went,

Stubbs whispered, "Ark! Ark-zaggerating," which I did not think so because of my ears ringing. But Stubbs flapped his short wings at the fire and puffed up the flames and smoke. And, do you know what, that lion was not as fierce as his roar. Because he started coughing in a scared way.

But then he tried to trick us with snarly fibs, saying, "Oy be a narsty ole RRRRobber ye know. And oy be a wicked ole RRRRRipper!"

Quick as a chick I said "Listen Mister Mountainlion, if you help us, maybe we can find a nice juicy mice pie or 3 for you, yes?"

No more snarls at all after that, just chew chew lipsmack lipsmack.

That is how we craftily found out:

1) a fox and small wolfcub stayed in a secret hideout cave last night

2) that same fox went HAR HAR about trick cutouts

3) that same fox said he was going to learn his map by heart and chew it up so nobody could follow

4) that same fox said to the small wolfcub about going across the border into Grimshire. To Hamneezia, the forgotten village.

Now guess who that fox and wolfcub are!!?

Yours aharly,

Little

Dear Mum and Dad,

Stubbs woke us up today going, "Ark! Ark-shun stations!" He was having a nightmare about getting lost. That made me get wurrid because of not having a map. But then I said, "Quick, Yeller, pass me the string off your kite. We are off to find the secret hideout cave where Mister Twister and Smells spent the night!"

Off went Yeller and me tunnelling. Stubbs stayed outside with 1 end of the string in his beak. Also I tied the other end to my tail. It was twisty work, but with our torches going flash and tugs on my tailstring from Stubbs, we never got lost, not once!

We were hopeless hunters for ages, then all of a suddenly I got a niff of baby bruvsmell.

"Arrrooo," I said. "This is it, the secret hideout cave!"

Yeller said, "YOU'RE RIGHT, LICKLE BECAUSE LOOK, BITS OF CHEWED MAP ALL OVER THE FLOOR!"

Just then I saw another clue, it was some more of that grey fluffy stuff like we found by Lake Lemming! We picked up the paper and the fluff, then I went tugtug on the string and Stubbs pulled me in like fishing. Outside in the daytime light I said, "Oh boo, this is not like maps, more like spilt ratflakes, now we will never find the way."

Stubbs said, "Ark! Ark-zammin, Ark-zammin!" meaning let me see. He tucked the fluff in with his other nest-liner in the rucksack. Then we found out why his label said he was good at beakwork. Because he got all the chewedupp bits of paper

and stuck them together with spiderwebs. So arrrooo, we are mapless no more!

Northeast is the quick way to Hamneezia from here. Pity it is over the Grim Mountains, they are a bit 2 high for small crows scared of highness. Still, he says he will go for the Arksperience, brave eh? Hope he does not get 2 giddy.

Yours readysteadyly,

Little

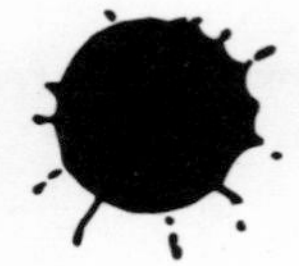

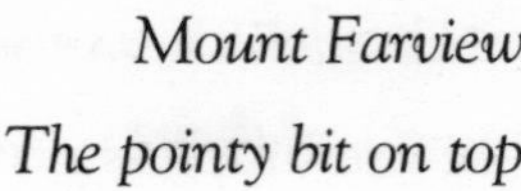

*Mount Farview*
*The pointy bit on top*

Dear Mum and Dad,

Off early with Stubbs snugged down in the grey fluffy stuff at the bottom of my rucksack. 3 Grim Mountains ago I said to Yeller, "I hate this high land, it is 2 hard on paws."

But up Mount Tester we went struggling. So slippy, but then we found new tricks for climbing. Plus Stubbs kept saying a muffly "Ark! Ark-cellent!", meaning well done. Mount Tester was a hard tester for climbing (get it?), hard up the south side, hard down the north side.

Then came Mount Skyward, about the same. But half way up Mount Farview it got 2 steep, the cliff started leaning out over us! I was keeping up with Yeller nearly, but all of a suddenly I lost my pull. I could not go up, I could not go down. My trembles made Stubbs pop out to look. I said, "No Stubbs! 2 highupp for you! Stay inside the rucksack!"

But he would not, he struggled out saying, "Arks Arks!"

I said, "Ice axe? Where?" and he gave me a small peck on the head. I said, "Your beak?" And that was what he meant.

So I took a trusting hold of his twiggy legs and UP I swung him. Then I gave a loud arrrooo for the best beak I know! Because it stuck in the ice like a bee's stinger in a bear's nose!

And that was how Yeller, Stubbs and me climbed the highest harshest mountain in Beastshire. All on our ownly we would be dead now. But together, slow but sure, we have done a Daring Deed like no cub or crowlet has ever done before. So into the Diary of Daring Deeds it goes, tick. ✓

Now we are the high-uppest campers in Beastshire.

Yours daringly,

L Wolf

*Hamneezia,*
*Grimshire*

Dear Mum and Dad,

Which was our worst, climbing down from Mount Farview or crossing the rope bridge over Perilus Pass? Answer, the bridge, because mountains are cold and crool but they do not wobble. Also rope bridges try to tip you off, AHHHHEEEeeee splosh! into roary water with sharp rocks sticking up. So that is enough writing about Perilus Bridge, it was bad as bangs nearly.

So I will say about Hamneezia. We got here after dark with snow floating down, v frozz and gloomy and glum. Nobody here remembers a snowmobile coming, they just forget everything.

Yours brrrly,

L

# Spooke

Dear M and D,

That Hamneezia was bad for branes, it made you feel giveuppish. So we ran off quick next day. Now we are in Spooke where the silver miners live. It is quite nice if you like old huts and piles of rubble everywhere.

There is 1 good game they have here. It is called Hello Ween and it is like this. 1st you must have some gloomyness and pumpkins with candles in, yum, tasty! Next what you do is, you dress up like a witch or ghosty or skerlington (cannot spell it). Then you walk up and down the street going woo. Then you go up to a door, knockknock. Then you say, "TREACLE TRICK!!"

And you get given yummy snacks to eat!

Yeller said, "COR, LICKLE, OUR PUPILS WILL LOVE THIS! LET"S BUY SOME BOGIEBEAST MASKS WITH GREEN GLOWPAINT ON. THEN WE CAN TEACH HELLO WEEN AT ADVENTURE ACADEMY." So we bought loads.

Tonight we are having a nice cosy curl-up. We want to get our strongness up for rescuing Smells.

3 woos from

Little

Dear M and D,

Oh no, Yeller is in bed with his tremblyest Snowtrembles ever! Here is the story of Y.

We were asking and asking for clues about Mister Twister but in a hopeless way. Then, nice surprise, we came to Bodger Badger's Garage and a cheery badger working there. I said, "Have you seen a snowmobile, a big shiny one with a propeller behind?"

The badger said, "Oo arr. Lemmy see. Oo arr. Snowmobile? Yerss, me dears. Stopped by here 3 days ago, oo arr. Nice old lady driver there was. Her hair was whoyt as snow. She asked me to fix on an extra big fuel tank, yerss she did.

And she bought an extra-strong roofrack and all. She had this big heavy iron box, oo arr. That took up too much room in the cabin, see?"

Stubbs said, "Ark! Ark-straordinary!"

I said, "Was there a small smelly wolfcub with this old lady?"

The badger said, "Dunno about no wolfcub, oo arr. She had her baby grandson with her, but I never did see his face. Poor thing, he had the chickypox. So his granny had to wrap him up tight all over ter stop him scratchin, see? Looked loik a little Egyptian mummy he did, oo arr."

I said, "But was he very squeaky and wiggly?"

The badger said, "Ooo arr! Ever so squeaky and wiggly!"

I said, "I think I know that squeaky baby. And did

the old lady smell of pepper by any chance?"

Answer, "OOOOO ARRR!!"

"AND WHICH WAY DID THEY GO?" asked Yeller.

Answer, northeast towards Yellowsmoke. "But oo arr, you don't want to go there on foot, me dears," said the badger. "Not across the White Wildness. There be no roads to follow, you know, nor no shelter. Just blizzards brewing. The worstest snowyest place on earth, that is."

That was when Yeller fainted. Now he is tucked up tight in Bodger Badger's spare room. Maybe he will feel better tomorrow.

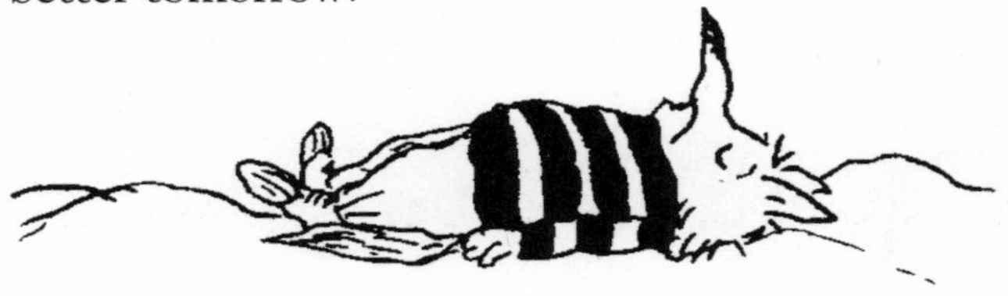

Yours hopesoly,

L Wolf

*Somewhere in the White Wildness*

Dear Mum and Dad,

Stubbs and me have gone on alone. We miss Yeller a lot. But he was 2 ill to come with us. Also he feels much shame to be a giveupper.

But I said, "Never mind, Yeller, some beasts do not like high places, some beasts do not like bangs. You WISH you were just normal and untrembly but you are not, so there."

I am writing sadly in a snowhole in the White Wildness. It is true about the whiteness, it is all white here, even the bears.

So no more now from

Little Wolf

Dear Mum and Dad,

Brrrrrr, so frozz, so weak.

Stubbs says all crows are Arksperts on going the quick way. That is why everybody says "It is 2 miles as the crow flies ect." Except Stubbs of course, he hates flying. Anyway, he says we are going northeast.

But I am not so sure. I have run and run today. But Yellowsmoke is not near.

I have dug a snowcave.

2 cold 2 write more,

L

*snowcave,*
*white wildness*

Dear M and d,

So tired   sore eyes   blizzard bad   trapped in snowcave

no food today   just lick snow   zizz   wake

sometimes I send up my Emerjuncy Howl for the wind to carry

But I am getting 2 weak

we have put out Yeller's kite to fly for a signal. Also Stubbs has done plaiting the string for strongness

the wolfeyes on the kite shine   but who will see?

From

*wit wildness*

drear mumdad, I cannot stay wakey only

dream of monster big growler

coming   closer            closer

Dear Mum and Dad,

Phew days since I wrote to you, sorry, it was the weakness.

About my dream, it was not a dream. It was the Snowmonster crawled into our snowcave. To take us away. Shiny blue body, blue head and buggy eyes. He was a terror but he came whisperingly. He did not roar, do you know Y?

Because he was not the Snowmonster, he was YELLER!!

He was wearing Bodger Badger's blue snowsuit! Off came his helmet and goggles and earmuffs. And there was his funny pointy face and his stickyout teeth, laughing. His voice is still not back to normal loudness, but even whispery it makes you laugh. He said, “SORRY TO KEEP YOU WAITIN. ANYBODY WANNA NICE FIGHT?”

I said ME! and over and over we rolled, the happiest wrestlers ever! It was a bit hot and squashy for small crows but soon Stubbs forgot shyness and joined in with some good rough pecks. That night we had a newsy Togetheragain Feast with yummy stuff from Bodger’s larder. Rabbit rolls and mice pies for me and Yeller, hmmm yes please. And Stubbs had his faves, worms on toast and crawlycake.

I will say Yeller’s news in my next.

Yours togetherly,

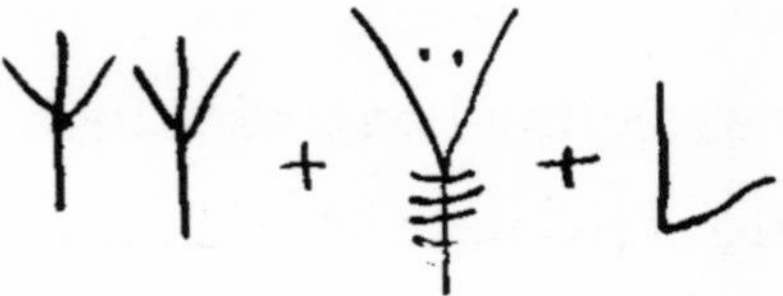

Dear M and D,

Here is Yeller's story. He told it like this, only quieter.

"WELL LICKLE AND STUBBY, THAT TIME YOU WEN AWAY, I FELT SHOCKIN. I FELT SHAMED. I FELT THE LONEST WOLFCUB IN THE LAND. I KEP THINKIN 'I MUST HELP MY CHUMS'. BUT EVERY TIME I GOT OUT OF BED I THOUGHT OF THE WHITE WILDNESS. AND I JUST FELL ON MY FACE, FLOP - LIKE THAT. I COULDN'T STOP FAINTIN, NOT WITH THE TREMBLES SO SHOCKIN.

THEN ONE LONE NIGHT I HEARD SOMETHIN CALLIN ME. IT WAS COMIN DOWN MISTER BODGER'S CHIMNEY. FARAWAY LIKE, BUT STILL CLEAR AS WATER. I SAYS TO MESELF "THAT'S LICKLE'S EMERJUNCY HOWL, THAT IS! HE WOULDN'T USE THAT IF HE WASN'T IN A DREADFUL BAD WAY!' SO UP I JUMPS, CALLING, 'MISTER BODGER, MISTER BODGER! YOU'VE GOT TO HELP ME SAVE LITTLE WOLF AND STUBBY CROW FROM DEATH BY BLIZZARDS!'

HE SAYS TO ME, 'ARE YOU UP TO IT?' I SAYS 'I'VE GOT TO BE!'

SO DOWN WE WENT TO THE GARAGE. MISTER BODGER GOT A BIG OLD MOTORBIKE, PLUS A BIG WHEEL OFF OF A TRACTOR, PLUS A SLEDGE. AND HE JOINED UM ALL UP TOGETHER WITH SPANNERS. AND BEFORE MORNING CAME HE MADE ME A SPEEDY SNOWTORBIKE! THEN HE GAVE ME HIS OLD BLUE SNOWSUIT AND GOGGLES, A BIT BIG FOR ME BUT GOOD FOR GETTIN MY BRAVENESS UP."

I said, "But still, how could you follow us? Our tracks were covered up quick! So how?"

"Ark! Arksplain!" said Stubbs.

Answer, "THAT CLEVER CLUE FROM SMELLS!!"

I said, "Clever? Do you mean that screwedupp paper with the wobbly C plus splodge plus yellow scribbles like this?"

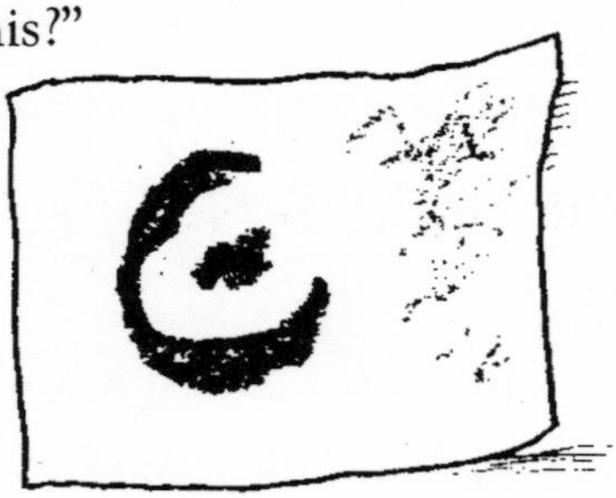

"WELL, LICKLE," said Yeller, "I FOUND OUT IT WAS NOT JUST SMELLS'S NORMAL DUNCENESS. NO, IT WAS A CRAFTY CLUE MEANING

C (SEE) YELLOW SMOKE!!"

So Yellowsmoke Swamplands is what Yeller aimed his snowtorbike at. And true the snow was a terror to him but he made the engine roar back at the blizzard. And at last he saw wolf eyes shining in the sky, and he thought, "I KNOW THAT KITE. I WILL SEE WHO IS ON THE END OF THE STRING!"

And he looked. And it was us, the end. Another Daring Deed for my book! Arroooooo. ✔

Yours savedly

L

PS Now we can rescue Smells, let's hope he is still ok, eh?

*Swamplands, the east bit,*
*not far from the Shivery Sea*

Dear Mum and Dad,

Fast riding makes you say to walking, "You are just a slow snail!" But oh for a snowsuit plus woolly helmet to stop cold ears!

Stubbs has got his grey fluffy stuff in the rucksack for cosyness. But I had to sit behind Yeller and hold tight. WISHWASH over snowbumps and cracks we speeded. We went so quick that now the Shivery Sea is just a short twinkling away. Going WAAAAAH! was a big help. But not having a woolly helmet, my face soon got frozz and my WAAAAAH! got stuck. When we stopped, I could not move, my mouth looked like a postbox for polar bears.

Lucky they have hot steamers in this land, they are like yellow smoke coming up out of the ground. Yeller and Stubbs had to lift me off the snowtorbike seat like a cardboard cutout and sit me in a steamer. Phew, goodbye frozz, hello warmalloverness plus my mouth going Yum Yum again for eating practiss!

Camping here tonight. Do not get wurrid, we will soon capture Mister Twister. And get Smells back, boo shame (only kidding, I miss him really).

Yours,

*The shore of the Shivery Sea*
*(north bit)*

Dear M and D,

Oo-er hot steamers are a danger when they get big as trees. You have to go along a wiggly path to miss them. But it is a hard 1 to stay on. So Yeller drove slow and Stubbs and me were sharp lookouts. But sometimes, oh no, missed the path! Then WHOOOSH. . . up we went like a pingpong ball on a waterjet and BONK, down in the squidgy mud.

No wonder flying is scary for Stubbs.

At last we have found the Shivery Sea, phew. It is grey and cold, like a big lake but more wavy. Plus it has pointy blue ice islands floating in it. Up we went northly along the beach searching searching.

But not 1 clue about Mister Twister boo shame.

Yours,

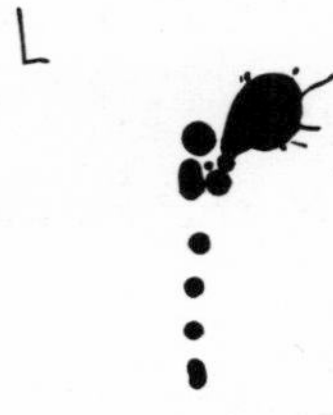

Noname Bay

Dear M and D,

South again by snowtorbike along the beach. Snow stopped but still no foxy tracks.

But clever old Stubbs spotted some grey fluffy stuff, then a bit more, and a bit more! It led to a rowboat full of holes. And in the sand right nextdoor to the rowboat was a BIG boatprint, plus scrape marks down to the sea.

Yeller looked on the floor of the rowboat. "OH NO!" he whispered. "SHOCKIN!" His fur was standing up on his neck. Because lying there, flat like a cowpat, was a small body.

All I could say was Gulp.

Yours dreadly,

Little

*Upsidedown Rowboat House,*
*Noname Bay*

Dear M and D,

Good news! That cowpat was not Smells! It was his ted with all the stuffing gone.

I am so proud of my baby bruv, even if he is a moany little scrooger. Unpicking his ted and dropping lumps of stuffing out of it for us to follow was a wolfly thing to do. Foxes think they know all the best tricks, so har har Mister Twister you never thought of that 1!

Spent today being boat fixers, maybe for a nice shelter. Also we had a good chat, so now we think we know where Mister Twister has gone with Smells.

Yeller said, "I THINK MISTER TWISTER HAD A BIG BOAT HERE. BIG ENOUGH FOR A SNOWMOBILE PLUS A SAFE, LICKLE. AND NOW HE HAS GONE SAILIN THE SHIVERY SEA."

But where xactly? Together we have made a strong new skin for the boat, with flatted out mudguards plus sledge bits off the snowtorbike. We buried the other bits. Also we have made oars out of tentpoles and picnic plates. Yeller's kite makes a hansum sail.

Your fixy boy,

L

PS Just now some crawly things came sideways out of the sea, and tried to pinch us with their pinchers. Handy,

because it was tea time yum yum. Bit 2 much salt on them but nice and crunchy.

Dear M and D,

Today we lawnched the boat. Or is it lunched?

We pushed it in the water, brrr frozz, so toes crossed for not sinking. It floated! I said, "You say a name for this boat, Stubbs." So Stubbs gave it the name *Ark*, just the job.

Sailing *Ark* was v scary, a bit 2 hilly for wolf cubs. But not Stubbs. He stood on the pointy bit at the front of the boat being the captain. Ups and downs did not bother him. I think it is a bit like flying but safe. His feathers are more bendy and black now, also shiny.

Me and Yeller did fast rowing to take our minds off sickupps. That puffs you out quick! Then all of a silently, up popped some nice nosy sea creatures, smooth as otters. Seals is their name, have you heard of it? We said our names 2 and told them about hunting for a cubnapper.

1 of the seals barked up, "Well mateys, all hands on deck and hoist your mainsail. Because we spied a big boat 4 tides ago. She was bound for Vile Island."

"Vile Island?" I said.

"Ark! Arksplain," said Stubbs.

"That's easy, me hearties," said the seal. "Vile Island is bang in the middle of the Shivery Sea."

Now the seals are giving us a tow, so must stop, 2 joggy 2 write.

Your queezy boy, Little

PS Just a short riddle, what makes yeller green? Answer blue, also boats (hard 1, eh?)

Dear Mum and Dad,

Dry land, I love it kiss kiss, even if it is all boring rocks.

The seals towed us all the way here. We went skimming past lots of blue ice islands (seals call them iceburglars, I do not know Y). They were all jumpy with penguins.

At last we saw Vile Island, it is a sort of a big black pile of rocks with a castle on top. And now we are on it (the island not the castle). So 1 more Daring Deed for my book, tick. ✓

Now I will tell you a proud thing about Smells. Yeller says he has been thinking about my small bruv's clue. It was a much more crafty 1 than we thought before even.

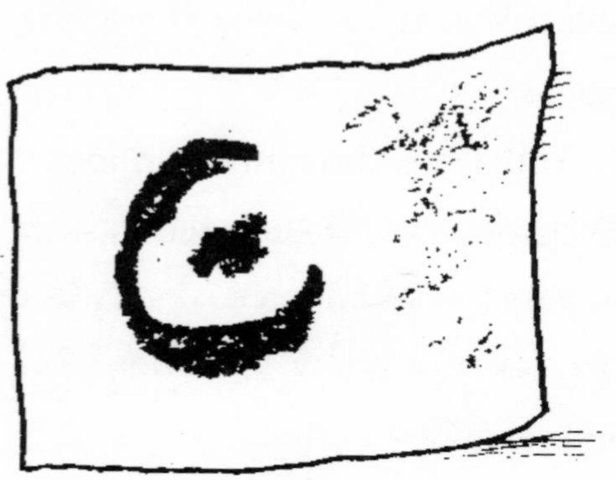

Do you remember that wobbly C with the yellow smudges next to it like this?

Well it was not a wobbly C but a SHIVERY SEA! Get it?!! It was a small clue with a BIG meaning like this.

*"Mister Twister is taking me to Vile Island next to the Yellowsmoke Swamplands in the middle of the Shivery Sea!"*

Who would think a small brane like Smells's has got room for paper clues PLUS trails of tedstuffing? Must stop now. Yeller has thought of an idea for getting inside the castle. Now we can really start rescuing!

Yours herewegoly,

L

*Vile Island*
*down the dungeons*

Dear M and D,

Um, we have found Smells but we have been sort of um trapped everlastingly.

1 good thing yesterday was a new word I learnt, "dungeons". Dungeons are what you fall down trapdoors into when you go creeping about in castles. Otherwise my news is rubbish. We have been foiled by that foul foxy tricker, boo grrr.

We were all going ow and rubbing our botts, then all of a suddenly, down came a peppery smell. We looked up and wayupp above, sharp eyes were looking down. Shiningly through the trapdoor. Next came a soft foxy chuckle and words. "Good evening, my boys, congratulations. I underestimated you. No one has ever found my secret hideout before. And now, welcome to my deepest darkest dungeon. Please pay attention while I gloat."

"You see, my boys, you have fallen quite literally into my trap. You can never escape. Smellybreff has proved, shall we say, difficult? My softest voice is wasted on him and he is too fond of gold to give in to rough threats. So now it is up to you, my boys. Either persuade the little brat to give me the combination of the safe, or you will remain here for ever. Here he comes now. Do try to talk some sense into him, won't you?"

Down came a cat basket dangling. Smells was inside with a gag on.

Then BANG went the trapdoor. Just to make me tremble, I bet.

Your shaky boy,

L

Dear Mum and Dad,

Still trapped everlastingly, boo shame, and Mr Twister has pulled Smells up out of the dungeons again. We just had time to say praising things like Good clues, Smells, you are a Daring Deeder! Stay chinnupply and keep saying nothing. Then he was gone again going mmmm mmm through his gag.

1 problem. If Smells keeps saying nothing about combinations, Mister Twister will get his temper up, I bet. Good thing you are zizzing while these shocking adventures are happening to Smells and Me.

PS By the way, Stubbs wants me to write that he is holding my torch while I am doing this writing. So thanks Stubbs, nice beakwork.

*Dungeons*. AGAIN!

Dear Mum and Dad,

Mister Twister came back to speak to us this morning but not with his temper up, phew. Only for a goodbye gloat boo grr. He says he has found a new way to make Smells be his friend again!

Because last night he told Smells a wopping fib. That he will let him be King of Beastshire! He says he can be on telly a lot, and all his subjects must give him their gold to put in his safe. Adventure Acad can be his palace and he can wear a twinkly crown and boss everybody about, even me and Yeller.

That fox is such a tempter. Now Smells will tell him the combination I bet!

And we will be in the dungeons forevermore.

Yours howlingly,

L

Dear M and D,

We just heard Mister Twister's boat leaving, oh no! We have tracked him all this way to save Smells, now we must get back quick to Adventure Acad to save him. But how?

What shall I do? My Emerjuncy Howl will not reach you at the Lair. Plus no post box near! How can I wake you up? Now who will go RAVING MAD at Mister Twister and save Smells from his power? How can we ever escape from this deep dark dungeon???

Ah wait, Yeller has just looked at me thinkingly. Quick, I must lend him my pencil. Toes crossed he has got an idea that wants writing down.

Yours rushingly,

L

*Vile Island, by the sea*

Dear Mum and Dad,

Arrrroooo! Yeller's idea was an escaping 1! So here is the story of the Daring Deed that got us out of the dungeons, a good 1 for my diary, tick. ✔

Yeller said, "QUICK, STUBBY, STAND ON LICKLE'S HEAD. GOOD. NOW, LICKLE, STAND ON MY HEAD. THAT'S IT. NOW STUBBY, TIME FOR SOME CLEVER BEAKWORK. TRY PICKIN THE LOCK ON THE TRAPDOOR!"

Stubbs fainted 2 times because of highness, otherwise easy peas. The next hard part was climbing out, but arrrrooo again for the Rescue Kit kite string, so handy!!

Off we went quick down to the seashore. But too late, that nasty Mister Twister had burnt our boat! Now we are macarooned.

Yours cutoffly,

L B Wolf and Co

*Vile Island*

Dear M and D,

Just a quick note but you will think, hmmm, interesting.

Being macarooned on Vile Island, we thought stuckly, ah well, what do rocky islands have for snacks? So we did rockpool hunts. We caught tickly things swimming like small commas with whiskers. They are v tasty, and the chewy stars. Also the flat crunchy things with pinchers we tried before, lots of those. Plus we liked the clingy things tucked up in their shells. Lucky Stubbs having a beak, much quicker than noses.

Then something happened. Like howling, but shivery and strange. Yeller found a broke drainpipe. He put 1 end into the water and said, "LICKLE, STUBBY, LISTEN DOWN THIS."

The sound was sea creatures calling. I put my mouth to the pipe and called ARRROooOOOOOoo!

Back came a call AYEEEEEEEOOOEE.

What can it be?

*Back on land in Grimshire!!*

Dear M and D,

Today I arrroooed down the pipe again and guess what, all of a suddenly black islands grew in the sea, 12, maybe more. They spouted water like Yellowsmoke steamers!

Then they swam right up to us in a pack. The leader put his wide flat chin on our beach and spoke low. "Who calls for a ride across the whaleroad?" His mouth was big enough to swallow a snowmobile.

"D-d-do you mean a ride across the sea?" I said all trembly.

"That is not the whale name. To us it is the whaleroad," said the packleader. "Our backs are at your service."

Down came his tail for us, a mighty 1 like a ramp. The other whales made a line in front of him. Stubbs hopped into my rucksack, Yeller gave a nod. And off we went across the whaleroad, running running till we crossed the Shivery Sea and reached the shore of Grimshire.

Yours puffed-outly

L

PS Big ✔ for a brilliant DD!

Dear M and D,

Still puffed out today and now camping yawnly not far from the River Riggly.

Whaleroad running was hard yesterday, also, quickmarching southly today. We must save Smells, he does not know what a tricker that fox is! So come on, Hazardous Canyon, we must get to you quick!!

Your racy boy,

L

*Hazardous Canyon (northend)*

Dear M and D,

We are so lucky having Stubbs, he may be just a small scaredycrow but also he keeps being a saver.

We looked and looked for bridges across the Riggly but no luck. So we thought ah well, cross it by log, here's one, paddle paddle. But no, that river was quick as a zipwire. *Zoooooom!!* we went, like a twig in a gutter. The rocks were sharp as teeth, lucky we missed them all, and on and on we went rushing, frozz and frit and tight clingers. Then we heard such a ROARING. We thought, Oh no, Funder Falls! Will we go H! E! L! P!

Answer, nearly but no. Yeller said, "QUICK, STUBBY, HELP ME WITH THE KITE. WE MUST SEND IT UP INTO THE TREES TO TANGLE!" Stubbs was doing his fastest beakwork on the cross-sticks then WHOOSH! ARRKK, come back, Stubbs! Too late, up he went *swoosh* right to the top of a tall oak tree.

Yeller and me held tight on the string and went heave till we came to shore at last, phew.

We got Stubbs down then, a bit trembly but not hurt. We kept saying, "Gosh thanks Stubbs, that was a Daring Deed. Stubbs, saved our lives Stubbs, you really flew there Stubbs!"

Stubbs just said a shy, "Ark! Ark-zaggerate!" Meaning that was not real flying. So modest.

Yours dryingoffly,

L

Dear M and D,

Yesterday poor old Stubbs woke up sneezy, saying, "Ah-ah-Arkscuse! Ah-ah-Arkscuse!" But no time for bed and glowworm gargle, we must rush to save Smells.

So big problem at Hazardous Canyon. There is a notice there. It says

Yeller whispered, "LICKLE, I KNOW THIS IS A SHORTER WAY THAN GOIN OVER THE DARK HILLS TO LAKE LEMMIN. ALL THAT SNOW UP THERE, IT MIGHT FALL ON US."

I said, "Yes I know and it might make a big bang."

Then Stubbs went, "Ah-ah-ah-ARKSCUSE!!!"

So Bang Rumble Splat down pounced an avalanche on us.

Yours stifflocatedly,

L Wolf

Dear M and D,

Shhh, we are secretly camping in Frettnin Forest. Cor, escaping from avalanches is hard. I was so proud of Yeller, he hates even touching snow. But Stubbs cawed, "ARK! ARKSCAVATE!" meaning no time for trembling, just hurry up and do tunnelling!

4 hours it took by hard claw and beakwork, no rest no snacks, nothing. But then out we tunnelled blinkingly into the moonshine. And pant pant arrroooo for our good old Lake Lemming, and watch out Mister Twister you cubrobber! Because 3 Daring Deeders are coming to get you!

Yours nearly homely,

L

Dear Mum and Dad,

Back at last BUT terrible news, the Adventure Academy sign has gone. Now the sign says,

Also we found chalky X marks on trees everywhere! Why does he want to cut them down? What is that Mister Twister up to?

Your wurrid

*Same camp as before*

Dear M and D,

Adventure Acad has got all new big locks and bars on. So up we crept peepingly to the kitchen window. And guess what we spied, Smells gagged up and strapped in his highchair! Plus all the gold on the kitchen table being chinkled gloatingly by A BIG SNEAKY FOX, BOOO.

Not fair, Smells was 2 easy to tempt being just a titch. He told the combination, just to be a king and a star on telly. And he never got his twinkly crown even, so crool.

But what can we do to uncapture him? Mister Twister has got loads more cunningness than us, plus all the doors and windows locked tight.

Yours hinderedly,

L

*Hollow hidytree*
*Frettnin forest*

Dear M and D,

Attacked at midnight!!

Mister Twister saw us doing spying, so he tried to kill us dead in our tent!

We thought we were tucked up safely in our secret camp. But no, BOOM!!! BANG!! my worst terror!! Down came fireballs falling slow, SCREAMING worse than owls. So bright! Even eyes shut did not stop you seeing

blue fireballs BANG

red fireballs BANG

green fireballs BANG

orange fireballs BANG

**BANG!!!**

I forget most of it now. Except rolling in the snow coldly. Then running running, more like a scaredy hen than a proud wolfcub. Then all was blackness. Then 2 wurrid pointy faces close to mine. Stubbs said, "Ark! Ark-splosion! Ark! Ark-cident!"

Yeller said, "HE FIREWURKED US, LICKLE. YOU BUMPED YOUR HEAD ON A TREE BUT YORE SAFE NOW."

I said, "Oh dear, sometimes I think Mister Twister is just 2 clever for us. What do you think?"

Yeller said, "GRRRRR. I THINK ENUF IS ENUF."

Yours shockedly,

L Wolf

*Hollow hidytree*

Dear Mum and Dad,

Yeller has thought of an ABCD plan. We have done A nearly. Which is, bending back small trees all round Adventure Academy. Also tying them down with string, then loading them up with snowlumps (like catapults, get it?!).

It was so hard and such a danger because of Mister Twister on the roof. If he sees us just twitch, he shoots rockets at us! He is a deadly aimer and he knows bangs are my worst terror. But I did not run away henly. I must be a brave Arksample to Stubbs. Because of Plan B tomorrow.

Dear M and D,

Tonight is up to Stubbs.

Yeller has told him Plan B. Plus he has done a banner to get his braveness up.

(Toes crossed for no fainting.)

Yeller and me are waiting in our hollow hidytree, ready for a fast race to the back wall of Adventure Acad, then tunnel quick into the cellar without Mister Twister seeing.

Stubbs is round the front now doing his job, keeping Mister Twister's sharp eyes off us. Catapult trees are ready all round, bended back and loaded with snowlumps.

So Plan B, you are on your marks. Stubbs the Crow, you must fly! Please fly Stubbs PLEEEEZ, you can do it.

This could be my last letter I bet. But you can still say "Oh well we are proud of Little and Yeller, because they did not half try to save our darling baby ~~pest~~ pet."

Farewell from

L B Wolf

*The cellar*
*Adventure Acad!*

Dear M and D,

We are IN secretly and that is 1 big tick for PLAN C, tunnelling! ✓ Yeller and me did tunnelling like 2 moles with a ferret chasing, phew pant. But question. Is Stubbs still a scaredycrow or a hero also? Answer, you will soon find out.

Plan B started with me doing my torchflash, our secret signal for Stubbs to fly quick and snip the catapult strings with his clever beak. But oh no! Mister Twister saw him doing his taxirun for takeoff. He loudshouted from the roof, "You foolish fledgling, you will never leave the ground! Take that!" Then he shot a big rocket right at him WEEEBOOM then more and more! Yeller and me thought, Oh no, he has exploded our cheery chum!

But then

arrrooooOOOOOOOOM!! LIFT OFF!!

Up went Stubbs faster than the rockets. He caught 2 of them in midair and pointed them back at Mister Twister going SCREEE-BLAMM! on to the roof. Arroooooo! that gave Mister Twister a sparky taste of his own shocks! Har har!!

Plus he was so busy dancing on top of the house, he missed us doing Plan C, busy digging down the bottom!

Now we must wait here quiet as slugs. Before we can do PLAN D.

Yours shhhly,

L

PS Good thing we did tunnelling practiss at Hazardous Canyon, eh?

*cellar*

*Adv Acad*

Dear Mum and Dad,

Da-dah, we have rescued Smells! Because Mister Twister has locked himself in the belltower to stop being bombed by snow and his own rockets. So in we crept to the kitchen and untied the small wiggler.

I spect you are really really happy and grateful now, saying Arrooooo for our Daring Rescue Boy, ect. But Smells did not even say 'Thank you brave bruv'. All he did was he bit me, just for taking his gag off. How did I know he likes going mmm mm mmm? Also guess what, now he says he wants to be a cubnapper like Mister Twister. We have to let him tie us up all the time or he howls his head off. And the worst thing, he has locked all the gold in the safe again and forgotten the combination!!

Mister Twister thinks we are still outside. We can hear him loudshouting to us from the belltower. Saying things like, "I know you are out there, my boys! But leave Frettnin Forest immediately. You will never stop me turning it into a Safari Park. Tomorrow my beavers begin cutting down trees to make room for the motorway. And in no time the hunters will be here with their loud guns. So BANG BANG you will be shot!"

Oo-er, better hurry up and do Plan D! We need some dressing up for it, also some cooking smells to tempt that fox down from the belltower.

So loads to do before midnight.

Your busy boy,

L

Dear M and D,

All set for Plan D and only 1/2 past 11, so time for a small note to say about it.

Yeller and me have got all our stuff ready:

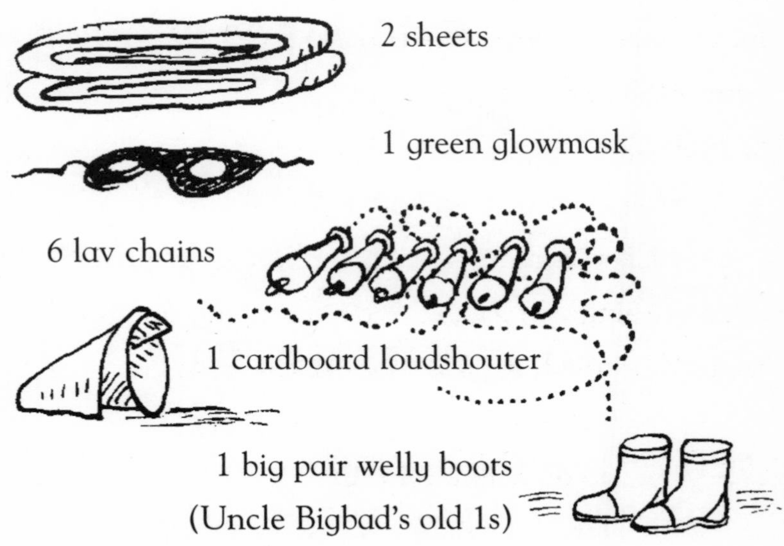

2 sheets

1 green glowmask

6 lav chains

1 cardboard loudshouter

1 big pair welly boots
(Uncle Bigbad's old 1s)

Also 1 cooking pot last 2 tins of bakebeans (canteen size, yum yum)

Just before midnight we will cook the bakebeans. Up will go the lovely smell. Down will come Mister Twister drool drool. Then out behind the curtain will come Yeller dressed up as a Bogiebeast. Also I will do a scary voice like this:

I AM THE GHOST OF BIGBAD WOLF

FLY AND FLEE FOUL FOX!!

SHOVE OFF TO VILE ISLAND

AND STAY THERE.

AND IF YOU BLINKING BLUNKING DON'T

I'LL BOIL UP YER WICKED BONES

AND SERVE YER UP AS SOUP!

Then Mister Twister will go oo-er mercy and run off. Good eh?

Yours craftily,

L

Dear M and D,

Plan D went a bit wrong, this is how.

The cooking part was good. Up went the bakebeany whiff, tempt tempt. Then down the belltower steps came Mister Twister drool drool. Smells was in his highchair, pretending to be tied up still. I was hiding under the table, also Yeller was hiding behind the curtain dressed up as a Bogiebeast.

In came Mister Twister quickmarch towards the cooking pot. In went the ladle, stir stir lipsmack lipsmack. I thought come on Yeller, hurry up, start shocking!

Then guess what, Yeller did not come through

the curtains, he came through the wall! And he did not have his glowmask on, he had a big furry face instead, plus great big red eyes and great big yellow teeth, plus all dribble dribbling down. Plus his eyebrows met in the middle like 2 furry caterpillars. Plus he looked all tall and thin and horrible.

Also he did not let me say my scary words, he did his own ones like this:

**I AM THE GHOST OF UNCLE BIGBAD!**
**ME WOT DIED OF THE JUMPING BEANBANGS!**
**I DROOL, I DROOL FOR A LUVLY GOBFULL!**
**FETCH ME THE SHOVEL AND FEED ME SWIFTLY!**

Mister Twister went white as a polar bear and jumped straight out of the window.

So I said, "Cor, Yeller, you were brilliant. You have scared Mister Twister away for ever I bet."

Only it was not Yeller. Yeller came out through the curtains in his Bogiebeast outfit. So I said, "Well who is that with the big red eyes and yellow teeth and all dribble dribbling down?"

And Yeller looked

and he saw

and he went "

AAAAAAAAAAaaaaaaaaaaaa!!

And so did I.

Yours oo-erly,

L Wolf

Dear M and D,

Arrrroooo, Mister Twister is really gone. And 3 arrrooooos for Stubbs! Because just as Mister Twister jumped out the window, guess who came flying through? Answer Stubbs the Crow! What a flyer, he loves it! He says it is Ark! Ark! Ark-zillerating!

Me and Yeller and Smells had all our fur up with scaryness when he flew in. He said, "Ark! Ark-straordinary!" meaning you lot look like you have seen a ghost. Which we had. Fancy Uncle Bigbad coming back from the nice grave I dug for him, eh? I spose he came back for a shovelful of bakebeans, he was always keen.

Good fun though eh?

Yours cheerily,

Littly

Dear Mum and Dad,

It is sooooo nice Yeller having his old noisy voice back. It was the shock did it for him.

We have been talking and talking about Adventure Acad. Yeller said, "KNOW WHAT I THINK, LICKLE, I THINK INSTANT ADVENTURE PLAYGROUNDS ARE FOR TAME PETS, NOT FOR BRUTE BEASTS LIKE US."

I said, "Yes, we like getting our braveness up in wild places, don't we?"

Yeller said, "LET'S NOT TEACH DARING DEEDS. LET'S HAVE ANOTHER SORT OF SCHOOL."

I said, "Good idea, but let us have a 1st Prize Day for our best pupil!"

Stubbs said a happy Ark! Ark-zackly! and did a looptheloop round the light.

Yours,

L

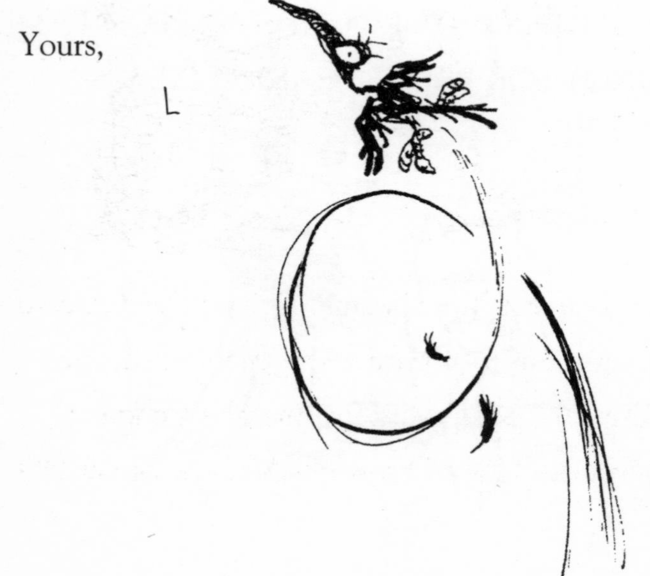

*Prize Day*

Dear Mum and Dad,

Today us Heads awarded our pupil Stubbs Crow the Adventure Academy Cup for High Flyers. His mum and dad were so proud, they brought the whole flock along to caw and flap him.

Then I gave Yeller his Gold Daring Deed Award for Braveness in a Blizzard. And guess what, the Gold Daring Deed Award for Braveness against Bangs went to L Wolf Esqwire. Also the Silver DD

Award for Clues and Courage While Cubnapped went to Master Smellybreff Wolf.

Shame awards do not stop small bruvs being painy and spoilt. He likes pretending to be Uncle Bigbad all the time, so he makes me feed him bakebeans with a shovel or no peace. So today I gave him a good bossabout. I said, "Behave, small bruv! Bakebeans all gone! Now we must buy more! But you have locked up all the gold. If you want bakebeans, just hurry up and remember that combination!"

No good me being Headly, all that did was make him be nasty to get me back. He is hiding somewhere, also he has taken the safe with him. When I catch him I will probly go RAVING MAD at him like Dad.

Yours gggrly,

L

Dear M and D,

I found Smells, he was in the garden with the safe. Plus Mister Twister's leftover rockets. He stuffed all the rockets under the safe and lit them.

Good thing I am a hero about bangs now. Because Smells's 1 went

**KERBLAMMM CHINKLE CHINKLE!!**

Smells says he only wanted to open the safe for bakebean money. He did not mean to blow small lumps of it all over Frettnin Forest, but a bit late now. It took us all day finding just 2 gold pieces.

Also he has blown his sailor suit off. Plus his tailfur. But do not fear and fret, Stubbs has glued him on some grey tedfluff for now.

Yours with ears dinging,

L

Dear M and D,

Good old Smells, he gave us a BRILLIANT new idea.

We will start up a new scary school for brute beasts. Our teaching will be Hunting and Haunting. We will do Hunting for Gold in the daytime, plus Horror Haunting in the nightime. We will play Hello Ween and have Midnight Feasts of bakebeans (canteen size). *That* will tempt back the ghost of Uncle Bigbad. So then he can teach us Walking Through Walls, Shocking for Beginners, ect. Also Stubbs can teach Spooksuit Making and Flying Lessons.

And Smells can be a small Horror and our new school will be called Haunted Hall, the Spookiest School in the World!!!

Yr xcited

Little

Dear Mum and Dad,

Me, Yeller, Stubbs and Smells are waiting for midnight. We have all got our spooksuits and glowmasks on. Also the bakebeans are going bubblebubble in the pot, hmmm nice. Uncle Bigbad's ghost will appear soonly, then the fun can start!!!

Yours spookingly,

Little

# HAUNTED HALL

## FOR SMALL HORRORS

Dear Mum and Dad,

I have filled Yeller's book right up now, so I am going to do LITTLE WOLF'S DIARY OF DARING DEEDS in all different colours on the front of it. That means now I am the bet winner, Yeller owes me 3 trillions of yummy grub! So hurry up Springtime and hurry up parents to come for a nice scary midnight feast. From now on the shocks are on me!

**AWHHHHHOOOOOOOOOOOOOOOOOOOOOOO!**

from

Awesome Animals
Awesome adventures with the wildest wildlife!
OUT NOW!
More Meerkat Madness
IAN WHYBROW
Meerkat Madness Flying High
IAN WHYBROW
Meerkat Madness
IAN WHYBROW
RACCOON RAMPAGE
HANG OUT WITH THE HOLE-IN-THE-TREE GANG!
ANDREW COPE
RACCOON RAMPAGE
THE RAID
ANDREW COPE

Awesome Animals
Penguin Pandemonium
The Rescue
Awesome Animals
Penguin Pandemonium
Little birds, big dreams
Jeanne Willis
Awesome Animals
Watch out for the world's wildest pandas!
PANDA PANIC
Jamie Rix
Awesome Animals
PANDA PANIC
Running Wild
Jamie Rix
COMING SOON!
Awesome Animals
Merry Meerkat Madness
IAN WHYBROW

'A gem of a story' – JEREMY STRONG

# Little Wolf's Book of Badness

IAN WHYBROW

Illustrated by Tony Ross

*Also by Ian Whybrow*

Little Wolf's Book of Badness

Meerkat Madness

More Meerkat Madness

Meerkat Madness Flying High

# Little Wolf's

## Diary of DARING Deeds